bushie dad
(note Big hat)

Footy

SHERRIN

WAVE

tongs

tap tap

My Dad

A Handy tool

For those Pesky Flies

A kangaroo rat

Sauce on Everything

D1264926

the Hot Sun

My Aussie Dad

For Graham, an awesome Aussie dad . . . and for all the other dads down under! - YM

For Huntly, a bushie dad who is a nice balance of all these dads. - GG

Scholastic Australia Pty Limited
PO Box 579 Gosford NSW 2250
ABN 11 000 614 577
www.scholastic.com.au

Part of the Scholastic Group
Sydney • Auckland • New York • Toronto • London • Mexico City • New Delhi • Hong Kong • Buenos Aires • Puerto Rico

Published by Scholastic Australia in 2010.
Text copyright © Yvonne Morrison, 2010.
Illustrations copyright © Gus Gordon, 2010.

National Library of Australia Cataloguing-in-Publication entry

Author: Morrison, Yvonne, 1972-
Title: My Aussie dad / Yvonne Morrison ; illustrator, Gus Gordon.
ISBN: 9781741692280 (hbk.)
Target Audience: For primary school age.
Subjects: Fathers--Australia--Juvenile fiction.
Other Authors/Contributors: Gordon, Gus.
Dewey Number: A823.4

Typeset in Kidprint.

Printed by Tien Wah Press, Singapore.
Scholastic Australia's policy, in association with Tien Wah Press, is to use papers that are renewable and made efficiently from wood grown in sustainable forests, so as to minimise its environmental footprint.

10 9 8 7 6 5 4 3 2 1   10 11 12 13 14 / 0

My Aussie Dad

by Yvonne Morrison

illustrated by Gus Gordon

SCHOLASTIC

SYDNEY AUCKLAND NEW YORK TORONTO LONDON MEXICO CITY
NEW DELHI HONG KONG BUENOS AIRES PUERTO RICO

My Aussie Dad is classy,
he wears stubby shorts and thongs . . .

He sings 'Waltzing Matilda', and other Aussie songs.

My Aussie Dad is happy,
playing cricket on the sand . . .

tap
Tap

Even if his time at bat does not go quite as planned.

My Aussie Dad likes thinking that his
barbie skills are tops . . .

Even if the snags have burst, or if he's burnt the chops!

My Aussie Dad likes camping in the bush,
so he can rough it . . . .

He'll fight the tent for one whole hour,
before he yells out, 'Stuff it!'

My Aussie Dad is sporty,
coaching footy when he can . . .

He shouts advice to all the players,
even from the stands.

My Aussie Dad, he's handy,
always busy DIY . . .

He really thinks the things he builds are truly dinky-di.

My Aussie Dad, when driving,
is always so polite . . .

Though he reckons he's at Bathurst when he's at a traffic light.

My Aussie Dad is certain
that he could wrestle crocs . . .

That's easy to believe when you're just watching on the box.

My Aussie Dad is cool and calm,
he never ever hurries . . .

Everything is 'She'll be right.
It's apples, mate. No worries!'

An Aussie Dad's a super bloke,
an Aussie Dad's your mate.

All I can say is 'I am stoked . . .

My Aussie Dad is GREAT!'